MY BOYFRIEND IS A MONSTER

A Match Made in Heaven

OR
WINGS OF LOVE
OR
LOVE IS IN THE AIR
OR
FLY ME TO THE MOON
OR
UNDER HIS WING
OR
UP, UP AND AWAY
OR
FEATHER KISSES
OR
WINGING IT
OR
I TOUCHED AN ANGEL

TRINA ROBBINS

Illustrated by XIAN NU STUDIO

with additional illustrations by YUKO OTA

GRAPHIC UNIVERSE™ · MINNEAPOLIS · NEW YORK

STORY BY

TRINA ROBBINS

ILLUSTRATIONS BY

XIAN NU STUDIO

WITH ADDITIONAL ILLUSTRATIONS BY

YUKO OTA

Graphic Universe™
A division of Lerner Publishing Group, Inc.
241 First Avenue North
Minneapolis, MN 55401 U.S.A.

Website address: www.lernerbooks.com

Library of Congress Cataloging-in-Publication Data

Robbins, Trina.
A match made in heaven / by Trina Robbins ; illustrations by Xian Nu Studio.
p. cm. — (My boyfriend is a monster ; #8)
Summary: Aspiring comic book artist Morning Glory Conroy is delighted to be in a relationship with new student Gabriel, but her best friend Julia needs her, Gabriel's cousin Luci keeps causing trouble, and other crises keep arising, making her wonder if the heavens are against them.
ISBN 978–0–7613–6857–1 (lib. bdg. : alk. paper)
ISBN 978–1–4677–0978–1 (eBook)
1. Graphic novels. [1. Artists—Fiction. 2. High schools—Fiction. 3. Schools—Fiction. 4. Angels—Fiction. 5. San Francisco (Calif.)—Fiction.
6. Graphic novels.] I. Xian Nu Studio. II. Title.
PZ7.7.R632Mat 2013
741.5'973—dc23 2012023872

Manufactured in the United States of America
1 – BP – 12/31/12

Chapter One:
Glory's Journal
Keep Out!!
This means U.
Property of:
Ms. Morning Glory Conroy
BUN

But you must have parents!
Everyone has parents!
Not me.
We Steamgrrlz arise fully grown from the primal stew.
sigh
MORNING GLORY! COME EAT BREAKFAST!
THEN WHO IS THAT?
MORNING GLORY! YOU'LL MISS THE SCHOOL BUS!
NNOOOOOOO

Unless I can stay home from school, I will never finish my comic on time for the annual D.O.G. Winter Festival! Ben and Lisa (why can't I call them Mom and Dad like everybody else's parents?) are so clueless! They don't even understand what I'm working on.
Hum!
OF COURSE I UNDERSTAND, HONEY. I USED TO LOVE UNDERGROUND COMIX. THE OLDER STUFF EVEN MORE THAN THE ONES THAT WERE COMING OUT WHEN WE WERE IN COLLEGE.
YEAH, ZAP AND FRITZ THE CAT! KEEP ON TRUCKIN'!
AND WIMMEN'S COMIX.
LISA, MY COMIC IS NOTHING LIKE THOSE!
WE KNOW, DEAR. AND YOU'RE BRINGING IT TO THE PUPPY FESTIVAL.
YOU'VE ONLY TOLD US A HUNDRED TIMES.
GROAN
NOT THE PUPPY FESTIVAL!
THE D.O.G. WINTER FESTIVAL STANDS FOR DO YOUR OWN GRAPHIC NOVEL. I HAVE TO GET STEAMGRRLZ FINISHED IN TIME SO I CAN GIVE A COPY TO YAEKO FUJIMOTO!
SHE'S THE WORLD'S GREATEST MANGA-KA, AND I'M NOT FIT TO SHINE HER DOCS!
I CAN FINISH IT IF I STAY HOME FROM SCHOOL.
YOU KNOW BETTER, MORNING GLORY. YOU HAVE TO THINK OF YOUR FUTURE. SCHOOL COMES FIRST.
Sigh

MY SCHOOL, SUNSET HIGH, LIKES TO BRAG ABOUT ITS DIVERSITY. AND IT'S TRUE.
HIGH
BUS
THERE ARE A ZILLION CLIQUES, BUT THEY MAKE NO DISTINCTION BETWEEN RACE OR CREED.
AND I DON'T BELONG TO ANY OF THEM.

THE MILLIONAIRE GIRLS CLUB! WHAT ARE ***THEY*** DOING HERE? THEY NEVER TAKE A BUS!

WHAT ARE YOU GIRLS DOING HERE? YOU NEVER TAKE A BUS.

MY MOM HAD AN EARLY SPA APPOINTMENT...

MELINDA

MY DAD HAD A GOLF DATE WITH A VERY IMPORTANT CLIENT...

MELISSA

MY DAD HAD AN EARLY FLIGHT TO WASHINGTON, FOR A MEETING WITH THE PRESIDENT...

BO-RING.

MIRANDA

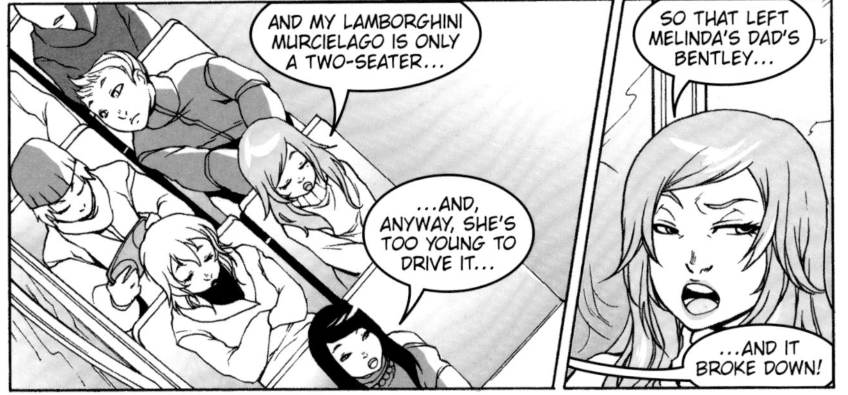

AND MY LAMBORGHINI MURCIELAGO IS ONLY A TWO-SEATER...
...AND, ANYWAY, SHE'S TOO YOUNG TO DRIVE IT...
SO THAT LEFT MELINDA'S DAD'S BENTLEY...
...AND IT BROKE DOWN!

STOP! YOU CAN'T SIT THERE!

B-BUT--

YOU GOT THAT DRESS AT A THRIFT SHOP, DIDN'T YOU? SO THAT MEANS IT HAS ***BEDBUGS!*** YOU THINK I WANT TO GET YOUR BUGS ALL OVER MY PRADA? GO AWAY!

DID I MENTION THAT BEN AND LISA PRODUCE FOLK CONCERTS? NOW THAT'S THE WAY TO GET RICH. NOT.

SO I GET MY WARDROBE AT THRIFT WORLD. BUT YOU KNOW WHAT? I LOVE IT! NO COOKIE-CUTTER CLOTHES FOR ME!

PERSONALLY, I THINK ***EVERYBODY*** ON THIS BUS HAS BUGS.

THOSE CLIQUES I MENTIONED? THEY ALL HAVE ONE THING IN COMMON:

DUMPING ON GLORY.

SUNSET HIGH SCHOOL

OH, GREAT! THERE'S THE SUNSET HIGH WANNABE GANGBANGERS, LED BY MARIO.
SORRY: "MARIO EL MAGNIFICO."
AW, C'MON, MAN. THAT'S TO CUT MY NAILS!
YOU'LL JUST HAVE TO **BITE** YOUR NAILS. THE KNIFE GOES.
SECURITY GUARD

YO, GLORY!

YOU'RE A GOOD ARTIST, RIGHT? COULD I PAY YOU TO DRAW A PICTURE FOR ME?
ME? YEAH, I GUESS...

I WANT YOU TO DRAW ME MADAME BAAAAD...
...NAKE IT.
Madame Baaad

AND WITH BIG GAZONGAS.
HEY, WHASSAMATTA? I SAID I'D PAY!
UGH!

COMIN' THROUGH!
ONE SIDE!
PERFECT. HERE COMES THE NEXT GANG: THE *GIRL JOCKS.*

HEYYY!
MOVE IT.
OH, MAN UP.
WIMP!
SPUTTER

AHEM!

MISS CONROY? MORNING GLORY? A MINUTE OF YOUR TIME?
ALL I *HAVE* IS A MINUTE. FIRST PERIOD STARTS IN ABOUT 60 SECONDS.
NO!
OVNIS EXIST!!
MISS CONROY. MORNING GLORY.
I'VE BEEN GOING THROUGH YOUR TEST SCORES...
55 SECONDS.
YOU TEST VERY HIGH IN INTELLIGENCE, BUT YOUR SCHOOLWORK DOESN'T MATCH UP TO THE TESTS. IT LOOKS LIKE YOU'RE JUST GETTING BY WITH PASSING GRADES. YOU COULD BE DOING MUCH BETTER.
YES, MR. BARRY.
OH, PLEASE: GARY.
50 SECONDS.

SO, IN CONCLUSION, IF THERE'S ANYTHING I CAN DO...

THANK YOU, MR. BARRY.

35 SECONDS.

...PLEASE DON'T HESITATE...

30 SECONDS.

NEXT.

20 SECONDS.

WHAT ARE YOU DOING HERE?

I'M A TRANSFER STUDENT. SO I'VE COME TO LEARN, JUST LIKE EVERYBODY ELSE.

BUT I'M--

RRRIIIIIIIIIII

10 SECONDS.

IINNNNNGGGG!

ZERO. FIRST PERIOD.

AH, MISS CONROY, GLAD YOU COULD FIND TIME IN YOUR BUSY SCHEDULE TO JOIN US.

PLEASE TAKE YOUR SEAT, IF IT ISN'T TOO MUCH TROUBLE.

huff huff

HI! WHAT'S UP?

UGH. FAMILY. I'LL TELL YOU DURING LUNCH.

Chapter Two:
Gabriel
IS THIS MR. JAMES'S FIRST PERIOD HISTORY CLASS?

HRM.

AH. ANOTHER TRANSFER STUDENT.

CLASS, THIS IS GABRIEL DIANGELO, WHO HAS JUST TRANSFERRED TO SUNSET HIGH FROM, AH, SOMEWHERE.
I'M SURE YOU'LL ALL MAKE HIM WELCOME IN YOUR OWN INIMITABLE WAYS.

GABRIEL, PLEASE TAKE A VACANT SEAT.
WELL, ***HELLO*** THERE.

HI!

SO YOU'RE JULIA ALVAREZ.
UM...
THAT'S HER. AND SHE HAPPENS TO BE ***FREE*** TONIGHT!

AND PERHAPS YOU'RE FREE TO OPEN YOUR BOOKS TO THE CIVIL RIGHTS MOVEMENT?
ULP
DUUUUDE, YOU COME FROM A FUNERAL?
A WEDDING?
A BAR MITZVAH?
OMIGOD, HE ALREADY LIKES YOU! JUST LIKE THAT!
DID YOU SEE CANDI'S FACE?

LET'S SIT ANYWHERE BUT THERE! TO SIT UNINVITED AT THE ***ALMOST LEGALLY BLONDES'*** TABLE IS TO MEET YOUR DOOM.

I SEE A SPOT.

SO YOU SAID FAMILY PROBLEMS?
OH, GLOOM. IT'S MY STEPDAD. AND MY MOM.

IT'S BEEN A PRETTY ROTTEN DIVORCE. MOM'S REALLY MAD AT HIM, AND SHE HAS A RIGHT. LET'S FACE IT, HE **DRINKS TOO MUCH.**
SO SHE HAS CUSTODY OF ESTELLA AND WON'T LET HIM SEE HER. BUT BIG AL'S BEEN HANGING AROUND ANYWAY. WE SAW HIM ACROSS THE STREET, LOOKING UP AT OUR WINDOWS.

SO MOM'S TAKING OUT A RESTRAINING ORDER. ***A RESTRAINING ORDER!***
ESTELLA'S ONLY TWO YEARS OLD. I HATE TO SEE THEM FIGHT OVER HER LIKE THIS!
I'M SO SORRY. I KNOW HOW MUCH YOU LOVE THAT BABY SISTER OF YOURS. IF THERE'S ANY WAY I CAN HELP...

YOU HELP ALL THE TIME, JUST BY BEING MY FRIEND.
HEY, TOMORROW'S SATURDAY! WE CAN DROWN OUR SORROWS IN...

...THRIFT SHOPPING!
OOH, LOOK AT THAT RED DRESS! IS THAT FROM ***SATURDAY NIGHT FEVER,*** OR WHAT?
AND YOU WILL WEAR IT EXACTLY WHERE?
THE JUNIOR PROM, IF ANYBODY ASKS ME.
SUNSET HIGH DOESN'T ***HAVE*** A JUNIOR PROM.
GOOD THING, 'CAUSE NOBODY ASKED ME!

WHADDAYA THINK? ***PRETTY IN PINK?***

GLORY, DON'T LOOK NOW, BUT-- ***LOOK!***

WHAT'S MISTER HOTTIE DOING ***HERE?***

T-Shirt

SHOULD WE...?

WELL, DUH.

MY CLOTHES ARE ALL WRONG.
I...I HAVE AN ALLOWANCE FROM THE FAMILY.
I JUST DON'T KNOW WHAT'S GOOD.
50%
WE'RE *EXPERTS.*
DRESSING ROOM
JEANS-MEN

YES?
YES!
MY OLD SUIT. A DONATION.
THIRFT WORLD
TIPS
THIRFT WORLD

THE PALACE
THE PALACE
HAVE YOU EVER SEEN MOVIES?
OF COURSE WE'VE SEEN MOVIES!

OF COURSE *I'VE* SEEN MOVIES!
I MEAN, HAVE YOU SEEN THAT ONE? I'D LIKE TO SEE *THAT* ONE TONIGHT. WOULD YOU LADIES CARE TO JOIN ME?
SHRIEK IV
THE RETURN OF CHARLIE

BOTH OF US?
AMAZINGLY, WE HAVE NOTHING PLANNED FOR TONIGHT. WE'D *LOVE* TO!

Odetta
IT'S NOT A **DATE,** LISA! THE THREE OF US ARE GOING **TOGETHER.**
Dum Diddyump Dum

MOM WAS JUST CALLED IN TO TAKE THE NIGHT SHIFT BECAUSE ANOTHER WAITRESS WAS IN A CAR ACCIDENT AND BROKE HER ARM, AND I HAVE TO STAY HOME WITH ESTELLA.
NO, I *INSIST* YOU GO WITHOUT ME!
GLORY, IF YOU DON'T GO, I SWEAR I'LL BE *FURIOUS* AT YOU!
IF WE BOTH FLAKE OUT ON GABRIEL, CANDI'LL GET HER CLAWS INTO HIM!
I WILL TALK ABOUT *YOU* TO HIM *ALL EVENING.*
BIG SISTER LITTLE SISTER

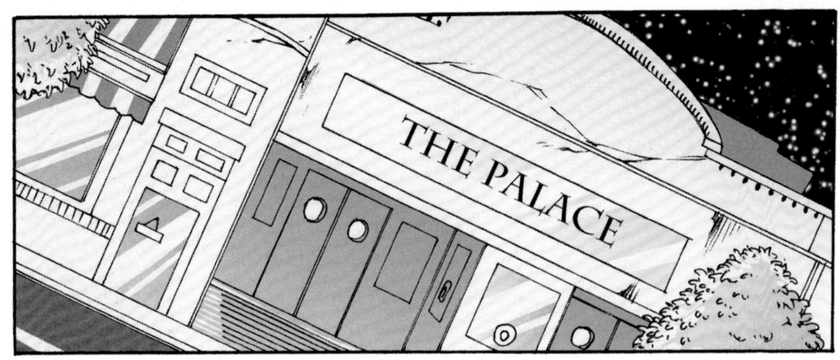

I WAS ***POSITIVE*** THE HOMICIDAL MANIAC WAS GOING TO KILL THAT GIRL! AND THE AUDIENCE--EVERYONE REACTED AS IF IT WAS ***REALLY HAPPENING.***

ACCEPTING ILLUSION AS REALITY. AMAZING.

BUT ONE THING: WHEN GIRLS HEAR A NOISE, DO THEY ALWAYS GO OUTSIDE IN THEIR ***NIGHTGOWNS?***

AND NEVER TURN ON THE ***LIGHT SWITCH*** IN A DARK HOUSE?

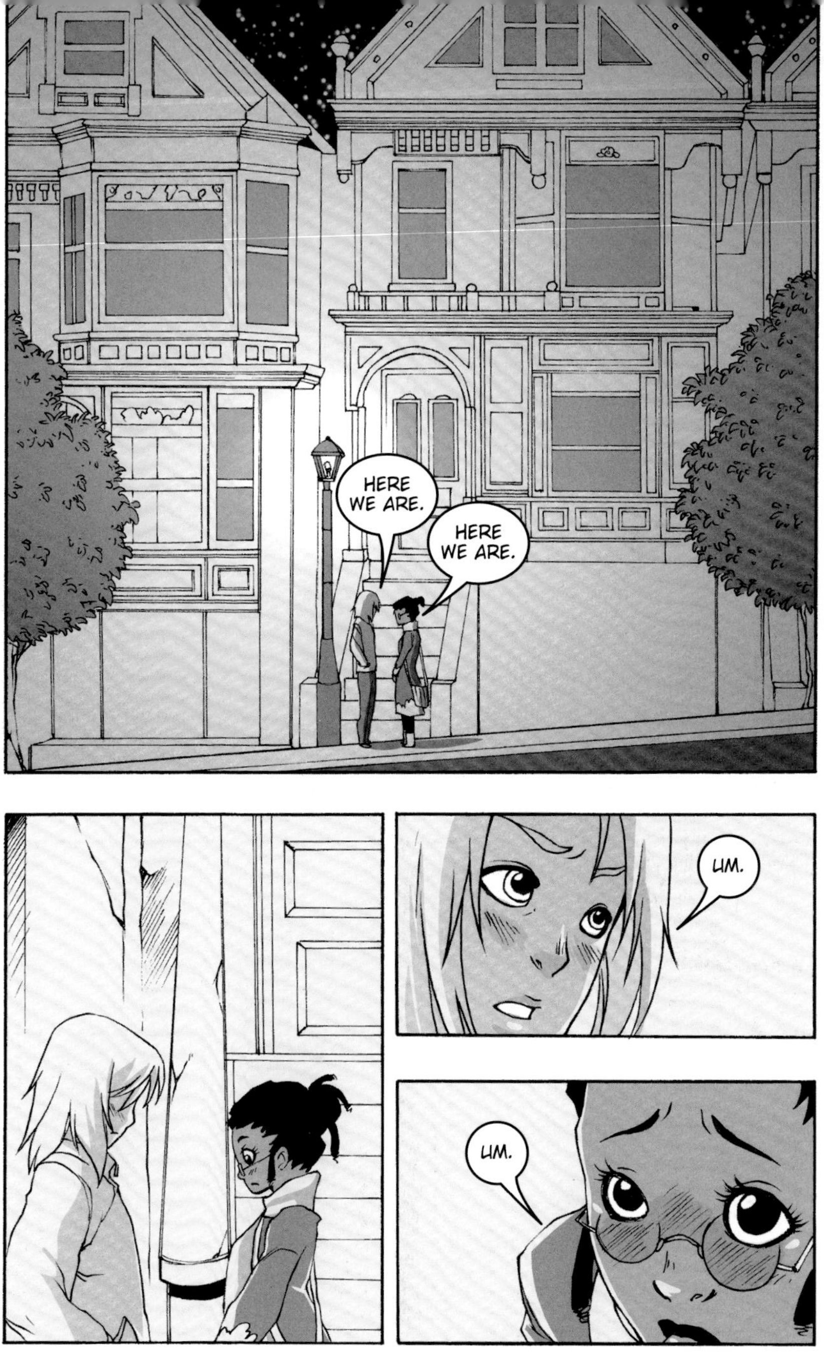

HERE WE ARE.

HERE WE ARE.

ok
I gotta go...

JULIA!

WELCOME
GOODBYE
JULIA!

Justin Pieiber
I'LL **NEVER** GO OUT WITH HIM AGAIN. I WON'T EVEN **LOOK** AT HIM...
GLORY, IT'S **OK.**

HOW IS IT **OK?**
GABRIEL'S CUTE AND ALL. HE'S **HOT.**
BUT THERE'S NO CHEMISTRY BETWEEN US.
MY HEART DOESN'T THUMP WHEN I LOOK AT HIM. I DON'T WANT TO WALK HAND IN HAND INTO THE SUNSET.

THERE WAS **SOME** THUMPING.
IF YOU FEEL THAT WAY ABOUT HIM, I'M HAPPY FOR YOU, **HONEST.**

SO YOU DON'T MIND IF HE'S MY BOYFRIEND?
HE CAN BE YOUR BOYFRIEND.

SUNSE
GABRIEL!
YES, I DID. YES, I LIKED IT. BUT I DIDN'T PLAN TO--
WHY NOT? BUT--
GABRIEL? SOMETHING WRONG?
MY GUIDA--MY GUARDIAN SAYS I CAN'T...BE PHYSICAL WITH YOU ANYMORE.
WHAT, NO KISSING? HA HA HA!
YOU'RE KIDDING, RIGHT?

EXCUSE ME. I HAVE TO TAKE THIS.
WOW, THAT RINGTONE!

BUT...
YES...
OK.

NO, I'M NOT KIDDING.
BUT-- BUT THAT'S RIDICULOUS!
ANYWAY, HOW WOULD HE *KNOW?*

TRUST ME, HE'LL *KNOW.*

BUT HE *CAN'T...HOW* CAN HE...

OH, *NO!*
OOF!

OH, LOOK. ANOTHER NEW TRANSFER STUDENT.

THIS IS, UH, LUCI DIANGELO. WOULD YOU TWO BE RELATED?
LUCI.

LU...?
LUCI. I'M NAMED AFTER MY UNCLE.
AND YES, WE'RE COUSINS. GABRIEL IS NAMED AFTER *HIS* UNCLE.
OH DEAR.

HI, CUZ!

WHAT ARE YOU UP TO? DO YOU HAVE *PERMISSION* TO BE HERE?
WHO NEEDS PERMISSION? I JUST THOUGHT THE *WHOLE* FAMILY SHOULD BE REPRESENTED HERE.
IF WE'RE FINISHED WITH FAMILY REUNIONS, PERHAPS WE COULD OPEN OUR BOOKS TO PAGE 97?

LUCI'S ALREADY JOINED THE ALMOST LEGALLY BLONDES.
LOOKS LIKE THEY LOVE HER.
I DON'T KNOW WHY, BUT SHE KINDA CREEPS ME OUT.
GABRIEL! YOUR COUSIN JUST GOT HERE, AND ALREADY SHE'S PRACTICALLY THE HOMECOMING QUEEN.
YEAH, LUCI WORKS FAST. PEOPLE GO CRAZY AROUND HER.
YOU DON'T SEEM VERY HAPPY THAT SHE'S HERE.
THERE'S NO LOVE LOST BETWEEN OUR TWO SIDES OF THE FAMILY.

SO, GLORY, JUST BECAUSE MY GUARDIAN SAYS I'M NOT ALLOWED TO *KISS* YOU...

...DOESN'T MEAN I CAN'T BE...CAN I STILL BE YOUR BOYFRIEND?
YES, I CAN FIT YOU IN ON MY LIST OF NO OTHER BOYFRIENDS AT ALL.

SEE YOU AFTER SCHOOL?
SEE YOU AFTER SCHOOL.

WELL, THAT'S GOOD, BUT... NO KISSING? REALLY?

I THINK BEING BOYFRIEND AND GIRLFRIEND MEANS MORE THAN THE KISSING SIDE OF THINGS.

BUT...NO KISSING?
WE'LL SEE.

So that's the sun!
It makes me feel all warm and happy!
You soaked in the primal stew too long, Steamgrrl. Welcome to the world.
You got me out of the gloom, Daisy...
HUG
When I rescued you from that treetop.
And you'll never leave me?
I'll never leave you.

Chapter Three:
THE WORST DAY EVER
RAINED LAST NIGHT AND IT MAY RAIN AGAIN. BETTER TAKE YOUR UMBRELLA.
UGH.
I HOPE IT DOESN'T! I'M BRINGING MY COMIC PAGES WITH ME.
I WANT TO SHOW MY COMIC TO GABRIEL. TONIGHT I'LL PRINT IT UP AND GET IT READY FOR THE D.O.G. FESTIVAL THIS WEEKEND.
YOU REALLY LIKE THAT BOY, DON'T YOU?
LISA, PLEASE DON'T START.

MORNING GLORY! YOU HAVEN'T, UM, DONE ANYTHING, UH, INTIMATE WITH HIM YET, HAVE YOU?
LISA, GIVE ME A BREAK.

I'M SERIOUS. REMEMBER OUR TALKS ABOUT SEX?
AND AIDS?
AND TEEN PREGNANCY?
LISA!
WE KISSED! ONCE!
...AND THERE WAS SOME THUMPING IN THE THEATER.
SOME WHAT?

RIGHT HERE.

HEY?

THANKS, NICKIE, I--
AND IT'S A CHEST PASS!
C'MON, NICKIE, GIVE IT TO ME!

ALLEY-OOP!
STEVIE! GIVE--

OVERHEAD PASS!
TERRI--

OOF!
FOUL!
BILLIE! SAM!
PTH

SMOOOSH

YOU DIDN'T EXPECT ME TO RUIN MY BLAHNIKS BY WALKING IN THE MUD, DID YOU?

WHISK
SPLOOSH
MY BLAHNIKS! RUDE!

OH, GLORY, I SAW WHAT HAPPENED! WHAT'S IN THE ENVELOPE? IS IT IMPORTANT?
THE PAGES FOR MY COMIC.
I'M AFRAID TO LOOK.
MAYBE YOU CAN FIX THEM.
MAYBE I CAN FIX THEM.

GLORY?
LATER.

AWFUL, AWFUL, AWFUL...

HAVE TO REDRAW...
...IN THE CIVIL RIGHTS ACT OF 1964?

NO, WAIT, I CAN WHITE OUT THE REALLY MESSED-UP PART OR PASTE OVER IT...
...CIVIL RIGHTS ACT OF 1964?

You got me out of the gloom, Daisy...

I ASKED YOU A QUESTION ABOUT THE CIVIL RIGHTS ACT OF 1964.

WHAT'S MORE IMPORTANT THAN THE CIVIL RIGHTS MOVEMENT...

COMICS! AND AN AMATEUR EFFORT!

WHAT COULD BE MORE IMPORTANT THAN SUPERSOMEONE FIGHTING ***MONSTERS?***

MY COMIC ISN'T--

WHO CARES THAT IN 1955, A TIRED BLACK WOMAN NAMED ROSA PARKS WAS ARRESTED WHEN SHE REFUSED TO GIVE UP HER SEAT ON THE BUS TO A WHITE MAN?

OR THAT IN 1964, THREE YOUNG MEN WERE BRUTALLY ***MURDERED*** BY THE KU KLUX KLAN BECAUSE THEY WERE TRYING TO HELP OTHER AMERICANS REGISTER TO VOTE?

BORING, RIGHT?

NOT AS EXCITING AS ZOMBIE-WOMAN AND WERE-BEAST PUNCHING EACH OTHER OUT, RIGHT?
BUT--
WHO CARES ABOUT HISTORY WHEN CAPTAIN MAGIC AND MUMMY GIRL ARE THE ONLY ONES WHO CAN SAVE THE WORLD FROM BLOWING UP?
WHY DID I BOTHER GETTING TWO DOCTORATES?

YOU THINK MADAME BAAAAD IS GOING TO SAVE YOU?
MR. JAMES.
I WAS IN A GOOD GRUNGE BAND IN 1992.
I COULD BE PLAYING THE FILLMORE! I COULD--
QUINN. STOP.
EH?
LET'S GO TO MY OFFICE FOR A CUP OF CHAMOMILE TEA.
MS. GONZALEZ WILL TAKE OVER UNTIL YOU, UM, FEEL BETTER.
W-WHAT JUST HAPPENED TO ME?
OKAY. THE CIVIL RIGHTS ACT OF 1964...
I KNOW WHAT YOU DID.
WHAT DID I DO?
ARE YOU OK?
I THINK SO.
AMATEUR EFFORT.

ARE YOU *SURE* YOU'RE OKAY? YOU DON'T *LOOK* SO GOOD.
IT'S JUST THAT...
...THIS HAS BEEN SUCH A WEIRD DAY!
CRAZY THINGS HAPPENING, ONE AFTER THE OTHER...
UM, GLORY, I DON'T THINK YOU SHOULD SIT THERE. THIS TABLE--
THIS TABLE BELONGS TO THE *ALMOST LEGALLY BLONDES!* WHAT WERE YOU THINKING?
HEE HEE
HEE HEE
HEE HEE
UGH!
BLIP

MY DRESS!

HEE HEE HEE HEE HEE HEE

YOU-- YOU--

DON'T DO IT, GLORY! SHE'S NOT ***WORTH*** IT!

I DID YOU A ***FAVOR.*** THAT DRESS IS A ***RAG.*** NOW YOU CAN BUY A ***NEW*** ONE.

TEE HEE

COME ON, LET'S CLEAN YOU UP.

I DON'T THINK IT'LL STAIN.
BUT IF IT DOES, CANDI GAVE US A GOOD REASON TO GO THRIFT SHOPPING AGAIN.
WHAT ABOUT THAT PAGE? CAN YOU FIX IT?
YEAH...

...I CAN TRY.
IT WORKS!

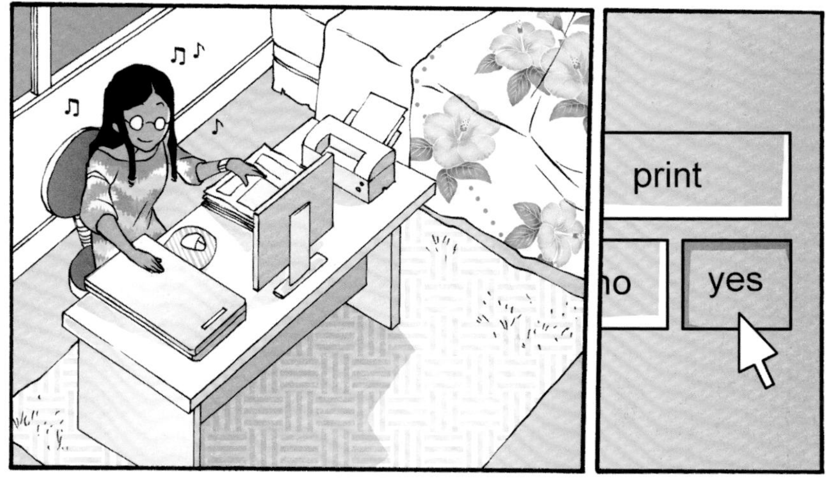
print
no
yes

ARGH!
KRK
RK
RK
Sorry! This piece of junk you call a printer is broken and will never work again!

COPY SHOP.

ZZZZ
ZZZZ

MERRY

BEER AND WINE
OH GOODY, MY FAVORITE THING IN THE WHOLE WORLD...
A BUNCH OF NEANDERTHALS DRINKING BEER.

BEER AND WINE

OH NO, **NOT** MARIO EL MAGNIFICO! IGNORE HIM.

HEY, GLORY!

OPEN

YO! YO!

HEY, WHY WOULDN'T YOU DO THAT **DRAWING** FOR ME?

TOO **STUCK-UP?**

I WAS GONNA **PAY** YOU!

MARIO, YOU'RE **DRUNK.** HOW DID YOU GET THAT BEER ANYWAY?

I KNOW YOU'RE NOT OLD ENOUGH TO BUY IT YOURSELF.

YO! YO!

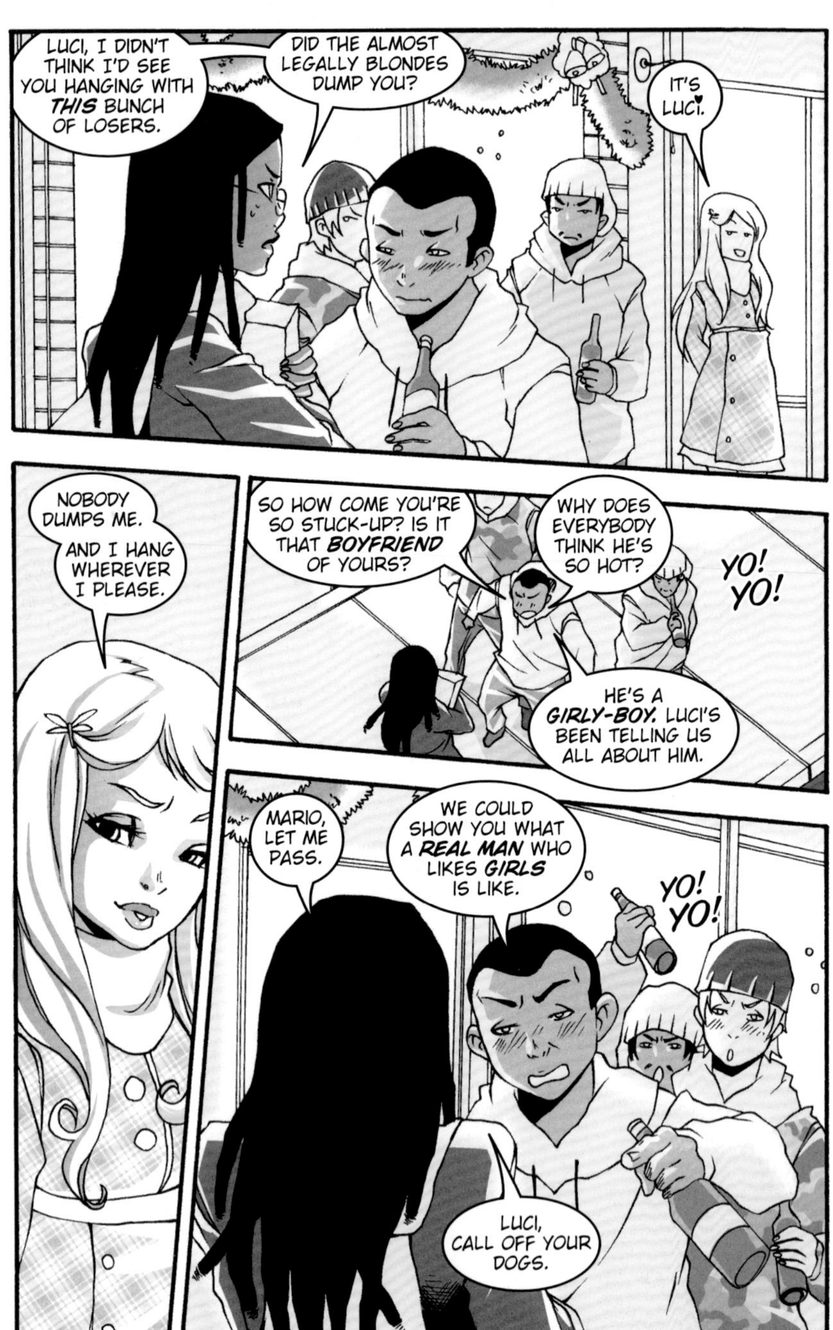
LUCI, I DIDN'T THINK I'D SEE YOU HANGING WITH THIS BUNCH OF LOSERS.
DID THE ALMOST LEGALLY BLONDES DUMP YOU?
IT'S LUCI♥.
NOBODY DUMPS ME.
AND I HANG WHEREVER I PLEASE.
SO HOW COME YOU'RE SO STUCK-UP? IS IT THAT BOYFRIEND OF YOURS?
WHY DOES EVERYBODY THINK HE'S SO HOT?
YO! YO!
HE'S A GIRLY-BOY. LUCI'S BEEN TELLING US ALL ABOUT HIM.
MARIO, LET ME PASS.
WE COULD SHOW YOU WHAT A REAL MAN WHO LIKES GIRLS IS LIKE.
YO! YO!
LUCI, CALL OFF YOUR DOGS.

MARIO...

GABRIEL?
HOW DID...?

NOT
HELL.

...THE
HELL?

HEY, THAT WAS *FUN,* RIGHT? TERRORIZING A DEFENSELESS PERSON?
NOW WHAT SAY YOU GUYS CALL IT A NIGHT AND JUST GO *HOME?*
YOU GONNA *MAKE* ME, GIRLY-BOY?
DON'T START THIS.
GET OUT OF THE WAY, GLORY.

GLORY, GET *OUT* OF THE *WAY.*
YOU GONNA *MAKE ME?!*

BY DOSE!
SMOOSH

HE *BROGE* BY *DOSE!*

WHAT HAPPENED?

I'M SORRY I PUSHED YOU, GLORY. ARE YOU OKAY?

I REASONED WITH THEM.

AWESOME, THEY'RE GONE. WHAT DID YOU *DO?*

UH-HUH.

WAIT... JUST A LITTLE SHAKY... I...

...IT'S JUST...

OH, GABRIEL!

THEY COULD'VE...

IF YOU HADN'T...

IT'S OK NOW. MAYBE SOME TEA, COFFEE? JUST SIT QUIETLY?

COFFEE

BETHANY'S COFFEE

BETHANY'S COFFEE

SNF

YOUR COUSIN...

DON'T WORRY, I'LL DEAL WITH HER.

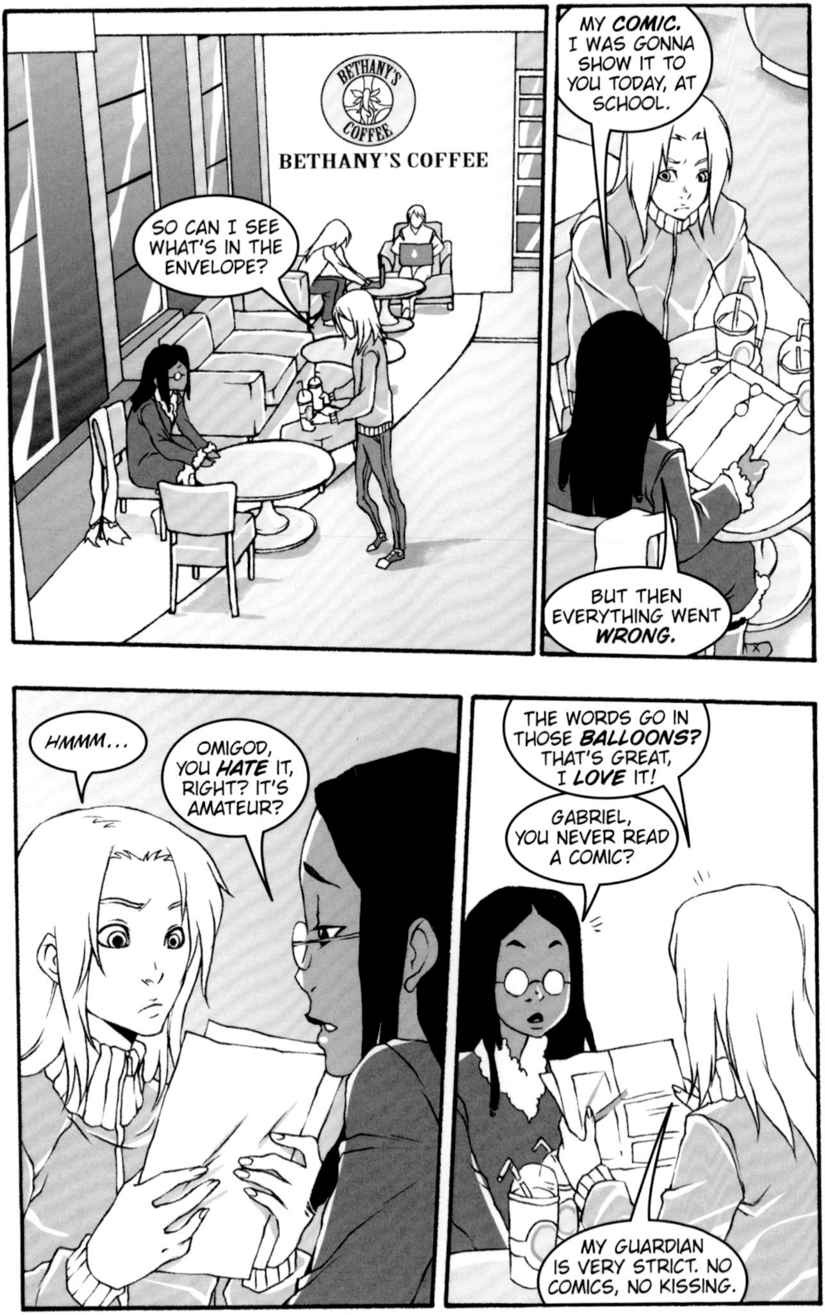

BETHANY'S COFFEE
BETHANY'S COFFEE

SO CAN I SEE WHAT'S IN THE ENVELOPE?

MY **COMIC.** I WAS GONNA SHOW IT TO YOU TODAY, AT SCHOOL.

BUT THEN EVERYTHING WENT **WRONG.**

HMMM...

OMIGOD, YOU **HATE** IT, RIGHT? IT'S AMATEUR?

THE WORDS GO IN THOSE **BALLOONS?** THAT'S GREAT, I **LOVE** IT!

GABRIEL, YOU NEVER READ A COMIC?

MY GUARDIAN IS VERY STRICT. NO COMICS, NO KISSING.

COME ON, I'LL HELP YOU MAKE COPIES.
THEY'RE *ALL* PRINTING UP THEIR COMICS FOR THE D.O.G. FESTIVAL!
FORTY-FIVE MINUTES FOR A COPIER.
LET'S LOOK AT THEIR COMICS WHILE WE WAIT!

THAT DOES IT. I'M OUTCLASSED BY EVERYONE HERE.
I'M GOING **HOME.**
NO!
HEY?
IT'S **AWESOME!** PEOPLE WILL **LOVE** IT!

AND IT'S **OUR TURN** AT THE COPIER!

HOW MANY COPIES ARE YOU MAKING?
UM, FIVE?
ARE YOU OUTTA YOUR MIND? YOURS IS SO DIFFERENT FROM THE OTHERS!
I SHOULD MAKE MORE, SHOULDN'T I?
FIVE HUNDRED!
I CAN'T AFFORD THAT! A DOZEN.
A HUNDRED.
TWENTY?
FIFTY.
OKAY, FIFTY. THERE GOES MY ALLOWANCE.
IT'S SO LATE! YOU'LL ONLY GET ABOUT FOUR HOURS OF SLEEP.
I'M GOOD.
YOU TOO.

GABRIEL...
WELL...THE D.O.G. FESTIVAL IS TOMORROW.
...YOU CAN KISS ME GOOD NIGHT.
I CAN'T.
I'M NOT ALLOWED.
I'M ALLOWING YOU.

WELCOME D.O.G.
STIVAL
DO YOU THINK THERE'LL BE KIDS HERE DRESSED UP LIKE SPIDER-MAN?
I THINK I SHOULD TURN AROUND AND GO HOME RIGHT NOW, BEFORE I MAKE A **FOOL** OF MYSELF.
GLORY, YOU'VE ALREADY BEEN TO **TWO OTHER** D.O.G. FESTIVALS!
YEAH, BUT THIS IS THE FIRST TIME I'VE BROUGHT MY **OWN** COMIC.

FREE HUGS!
WORRIED BUNNY
GLORY, THERE ARE **REAL PUBLISHERS** HERE! MAYBE ONE OF THEM WILL PUBLISH YOUR COMIC!
THERE'S **WORRIED BUNNY!**

PEACHIES
PRESS
CHEESSI
Sing with US!!
MIKE
JOHN

PLEEEEZE COME WITH ME, JULIA! I'LL BE YOUR BFF!
YOU'RE ALREADY MY BFF.
HIES
ESS

I CAN COME WITH YOU, GLORY.
I'D RATHER DIE THAN HAVE YOU SEE ME MAKING A FOOL OF MYSELF.
GO... GO LOOK AT COMICS!

I'LL STAND BEHIND YOU. BUT YOU'RE GONNA DO THIS YOURSELF, RIGHT?
HIES
ESS

PEACHIES PRESS IS A VERY SMALL PRESS. IN FACT, PEACHIES PRESS IS JUST ME.
PEACHIES PRESS ONLY PUBLISHES ONE COMIC, PEACHIES COMICS, DRAWN BY ME.
SWAP? HERE'S A FREE COPY.
THANKS.

KAWAII! THIS IS SUPERCUTE!
YOU NEED TO PUT YOUR COMIC UP ONLINE, LIKE WE DO. A PAGE A DAY.
THEN WHEN WE HAVE ENOUGH PAGES, WE TURN IT INTO A BOOK.
LOLITA
LOLITA
LOLITA
LOLITA
LOLITA
LOLITA

HERE, TAKE A FREE COPY.
THANKS.
I'VE BEEN SELF-PUBLISHING CAPTAIN MOONWALKER FOR FIVE YEARS. A COUPLE MORE YEARS AND SOME MAJOR PUBLISHER'S GONNA GET INTERESTED, I KNOW.

GLORY...
HERE, HAVE A FREE COPY.
THANKS.
MY GIRLFRIEND'S COMIC. SHE'S VERY TALENTED.
SHE'S LOOKING FOR A PUBLISHER.

NOBODY'S GONNA *PUBLISH* ME, BUT I'M GETTING SOME NICE FREE COMICS.

GLORY, I GOTTA GO.

THAT WAS MY MOM. SHE HAS TO TAKE THE OTHER SHIFT AGAIN, SO I HAVE TO MIND ESTELLA. AND BIG AL'S BEEN PHONING HER ALL DAY, SO SHE'S ALL UPSET ANYWAY...

OH, JULIA! DO YOU WANT ME TO COME WITH YOU?

NO, YOU STAY WITH GABRIEL, HAVE A GOOD TIME.

ANYWAY, THERE'S--

YAEKO FUJIMOTO!
OMIGOD, OMIGOD!
KATHUMP KATHUMP

I JUST LOVE ***SUNSHINE HEARTS!*** IT'S THE BEST MANGA I'VE EVER READ.

YOUR DRAWING IS BEAUTIFUL!

I LOVE THE DRESSES YOU DESIGN FOR ***CHIZIKO!*** AND ***ANDO*** IS SO HANDSOME!

CHIZIKO ISN'T REALLY GONNA ***DIE,*** IS SHE? CAN ANDO SAVE HER?

HMM

YAEKO FUJIMOTO

YOU'RE BABBLING.

YOUR COMIC IS CUTE.

IT'S... KAWAII.
I LIKE IT.
REALLY?!

I'M GOING UP TO MY ROOM FOR A TEA BREAK NOW. WOULD YOU LIKE TO COME WITH ME? WE CAN TALK ABOUT **STEAMGRRL.**
TEA?
WITH **YOU?**
WOULD I **LIKE...?**

GABRIEL. I FORGOT GABRIEL.
JUST ONE MINUTE, YAEKO-SAN!

LOOK, IT'S GODZILLA VERSUS MEGA-BOY.
OMIGOD, **YAEKO FUJIMOTO** LIKES **STEAMGRRL!**
SHE INVITED ME UP TO HER ROOM FOR TEA!
THAT'S **AWESOME,** GLORY. GO, HAVE A GOOD TIME. I'LL KEEP SHOWING YOUR COMIC AROUND HERE.

I WON'T BE LONG!
SHE'LL PROBABLY TAKE A CLOSER LOOK AND DECIDE SHE **HATES** IT.

I PHONED ROOM SERVICE.

ROOM SERVICE!
OOH, WHAT A GREAT ROOM!
THAT WAS FAST.

THANK YOU. HERE, PLEASE.
AWESOME! THE CONVENTION GAVE YOU A *SUITE!*

WON'T YOU TAKE A SEAT? I'LL CUT THE...

I'LL... CUT...

I'LL... *CUT...*

OH, LOOK! THAT'S THE GOLDEN GATE BRIDGE.
HAVE YOU SEEN IT YET?
I BET YOU CAN SEE IT FROM THE BALCONY. WE'RE SO HIGH UP!
WOW, YOU CAN SEE ALL OF SAN FRANCISCO!
OH, LOOK DOWN THERE! THE PEOPLE LOOK LIKE...

KARRONK
...ANTS.
TIP
THUNK
HEY...

AAAAAAAAAAAY!!!

thff

ARE YOU OK?

YOU HAD WINGS!
DID NOT.
DID TOO!
WHAT ARE YOU?
CAN'T YOU GUESS?

A...A SUPERHERO!
NO.

A FAIRY?
NO.

DIANGELO? AN...AN...
NO.

NO WAY!

WAY.

Chapter Four: The Worst Day Ever

BETHANY'S COFFEE

BUT IF YOU'RE AN *ANG--*

SSHH!

1
2
3
4

TELL ME WHICH RELIGION HAS IT RIGHT?

WE WERE HERE BEFORE THERE WAS *ANY* RELIGION.
WELL...NOT *ME.* I'M... NEW. SEVENTEEN YEARS, JUST LIKE YOU. SO'S MY COUSIN, LUCI.
AND WHAT *ABOUT* YOUR COUSIN? LUCI'S NOT VERY ANGELIC. SHE'S JUST ANOTHER MEAN GIRL.
SORRY.
IT'S A LONG STORY...

WE'VE EXISTED AS LONG AS MORTALS. OUR PURPOSE IS TO HELP MORTALS, TO GUIDE AND COUNSEL AND PROTECT THEM. WE'RE SUPPOSED TO BE PERFECT CREATURES.

BUT WE WERE NOT PERFECT CREATURES. SOME OF US RESENTED HELPING MORTALS.
WE ARE BETTER THAN MORTALS, SO MUCH WISER!
IF THEY CANNOT SUCCEED ON THEIR OWN, WHY SHOULD WE HELP? SURVIVAL OF THE FITTEST.
THEY SHOULD BE WORSHIPING US!
AND THEY WANTED TO DESERT HUMANITY.
BUT THAT WOULD HAVE BEEN TO DENY OUR VERY PURPOSE.

AND SO WE FOUGHT.

IT WAS A TERRIBLE THING! WE ARE MEANT TO LOVE AND NURTURE, NOT TO DESTROY. AND YET, TO PROTECT THE MORTALS WE HAD TO DESTROY OUR OWN KIN. MY UNCLE AND HIS SIBLINGS LED THE FORCES OF THE PROTECTORS. LUCI'S UNCLE LED THE OPPOSITION.

IN THE END, MY UNCLE'S FORCES, THE PROTECTORS, WON. BUT IT WAS A *TERRIBLE VICTORY.*
THE OPPOSING FORCES HAD TO LEAVE. THEY WENT TO A PLACE AS SAD AS THEIR SOULS, AND THERE THEY DWELL, ALONG WITH LUCI'S UNCLE.
LUCI SAID SHE'S NAMED AFTER HER *UNCLE?*
"UNCLE." YES.
oh.

SHE CAN'T HURT YOU NOW. SHE'S LOST HER POWER.
I'M NOT AFRAID ANYMORE.
THAT'S WHY SHE CAN'T HURT YOU.

WHY DON'T YOU MIND YOUR OWN BUSINESS? YOU'RE NOT LETTING ME HAVE ANY FUN!
YOU SEE, LUCI'S UNCLE HATES MY UNCLE, SO SHE HATES ME.
IT'S LUCÌ, DAMN YOU!

LUCI COULDN'T HURT ME, BUT SHE COULD HURT THE GIRL I ***LOVE.***
SO SHE'S HAD IT IN FOR YOU SINCE SHE CAME HERE.
ALL THOSE PEOPLE--CANDI, MR. QUINN, MARIO, YAEKO FUJIMOTO--THEY WERE ALL ***BESPELLED*** BY LUCI.
IT'S ***LUCÌ! LUCÌ!***

EH?
GAHH! THAT ***NOISE!***

YOU TOLD!
AND NOW THEY'RE SENDING ME BACK!
I SAID I WOULD. YOU DIDN'T HAVE PERMISSION TO INTERFERE WITH ME. EVEN YOUR LAND HAS RULES.
YOUR UNCLE DOESN'T LIKE TO BE DISOBEYED.
AND WHEN HE GETS MAD, HE GETS MUCH MADDER THAN MY UNCLE.
MY-- MY FACE!
ONOOOOO!
SWOOP

IS--
IS THAT
LUCI?
NO, THAT'S
LUCI'S SOUL.
I DIDN'T
KNOW ANGELS
HAD SOULS.
GLORY, ANGELS ARE
ALL SOUL.

NO, NO, GABRIEL! ON THE TREE! ON THE *TREE!*
I CAN'T BELIEVE HE'S NEVER TRIMMED A TREE BEFORE. WHERE HAS HE *BEEN?*
YOU'D BE SURPRISED.
Chapter Five:
THE WIND BENEATH HIS WINGS
OMIGOD, MY PARENTS *LIKE* YOU!
I LIKE THEM TOO.
GABRIEL...
YOU'RE TALL ENOUGH TO DO THIS WITHOUT A STEPLADDER. COULD YOU HANG THIS ON THE HIGHEST BRANCH?
HA HA HA!
WHAT'S SO *FUNNY?*
EVERY TIME A BELL RINGS, IT MEANS AN ANGEL HAS GOTTEN HIS WINGS.
THAT'S NOT TRUE! THAT'S NOT THE WAY IT WORKS *AT ALL.*
GABRIEL, HOW COULD YOU *POSSIBLY* KNOW THAT?

EARRINGS FOR LISA AND SWEATER FOR BEN.

GLORY, HOW LONG HAVE YOU BEEN GIVING YOUR DAD SWEATERS FOR CHRISTMAS?
HUH? I DUNNO.
SINCE I WAS OLD ENOUGH TO BUY CHRISTMAS PRESENTS, I GUESS.

WHAT ABOUT GETTING EARRINGS FOR YOUR *DAD* THIS YEAR?
FOR ***BEN?*** YOU'VE GOTTA BE KIDDING!

BEN HAS ***PIERCED EARS.***
ONCE UPON A TIME, HE WORE EARRINGS.

HMM...

WHAT YOU SAID ABOUT LUCI THE OTHER DAY?

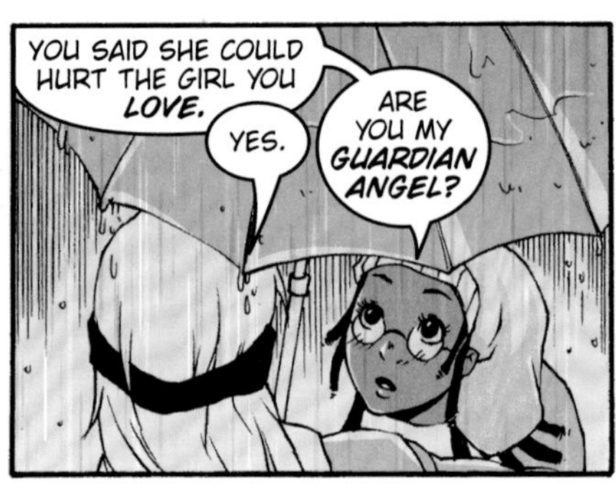
YOU SAID SHE COULD HURT THE GIRL YOU **LOVE.**
YES.
ARE YOU MY **GUARDIAN ANGEL?**

NO.
ACTUALLY, I WAS SENT DOWN HERE TO BE **JULIA'S** GUARDIAN ANGEL.

JULIA'S...?

YOU WERE DOING **FINE.**
AT LEAST UNTIL LUCI SHOWED UP. AND THAT WAS MY FAULT.

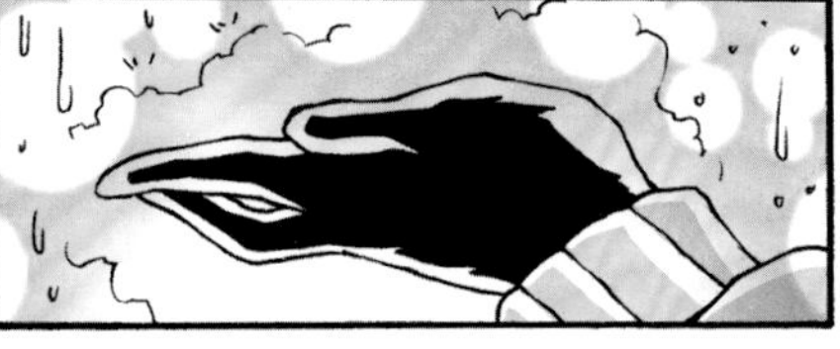

BUT I DIDN'T KNOW I'D MEET YOU.
I WASN'T **SUPPOSED** TO FALL IN LOVE WITH YOU.

BUT WHAT ABOUT JULIA? YOU SAID SHE NEEDED YOUR HELP.
I THINK **YOU** CAN HELP JULIA MORE THAN **I** EVER COULD.

ACT TODAY AND WE'LL THROW IN THIS SET OF NINJA KITCHEN KNIVES...
I WASN'T SUPPOSED TO FALL IN LOVE WITH YOU.
deet deet deedle deet
deet deet boop
...message is for Glory. This is Yaeko Fujimoto. Please phone me when you get the chance. My number is--
YAEKO-SAN?!

I CAN'T REMEMBER WHAT HAPPENED AFTER I INVITED YOU TO HAVE TEA WITH ME. THE NEXT THING I KNEW, I WAS ON THE BALCONY OF MY HOTEL ROOM WITH A TERRIBLE HEADACHE.
BUT IF I WAS RUDE, I WANT TO APOLOGIZE.
I'M TEACHING A WORKSHOP TOMORROW IN BERKELEY.
I'd like to invite you to come as my guest.
OMIGOD.
THEY'LL ALL BE OLDER THAN ME.
DAILY SF

THEY'LL ALL BE BETTER THAN ME.
comic workshop
SO, WHEN I BEGAN ***SUNSHINE HEARTS*** TWENTY YEARS AGO, I DREW MISS CHIZIKO TO LOOK ***MUCH YOUNGER.***
BUT SINCE THEN, SHE HAS GROWN UP SO THAT SHE CAN HAVE A ROMANCE WITH ANDO.

THEY'RE ALL BETTER THAN ME.

THIS PAGE IS AWFUL.

HEY, THAT PAGE IS AWESOME!
YOU *LIKE* IT?
WELL, ***YEAH.*** I WISH I COULD DRAW GIRLS AS GOOD AS THAT.

I'M DYLAN RUIZ, I--
HMMM...

YES, I LIKE HER EXPRESSION. AND YOUR METHOD OF DRAWING HAIR, VERY ***CLEVER.***

I THINK YOU'D LIKE THIS, GABRIEL. EVERY CHRISTMAS EVE WE GO CAROLING.
OLD SONGS THAT NOBODY REMEMBERS.
TO REMIND FOLKS THAT THERE'S SOMETHING OUT THERE BESIDES RUDOLPH THE RED-NOSED REINDEER.
THANK YOU, BUT A MOVIE I LIKE IS ON--THE ONE WHERE THE ANGEL GETS HIS WINGS.
SO THEY LIKED MY COMIC! AND YAEKO LIKED IT TOO!
YOU ONLY TOLD ME FIVE TIMES.
HERE COMES THE PART I LIKE!
EVERY TIME A BELL RINGS...
DINGDING!
UH?!
IT'S THE DOORBELL. I'LL GET IT.

MRS. ALVAREZ? JULIA? WHAT--?

OH, GLORY, IT'S TERRIBLE!

IT'S BIG AL. HE GOT DRUNK AND FORCED HIS WAY INTO THE APARTMENT. MOM TRIED TO PUSH HIM OUT, AND HE HIT HER.
HE ACTUALLY HIT HER.
THANKS.
sniff

AND THEN HE TOOK ESTELLA!
GLORY, HE TOOK MY BABY SISTER!
OH NO!

WHERE DID HE TAKE HER?
WE DON'T KNOW! WE TRIED CALLING HIS CELL...
HE CAN SEE IT'S US. HE WON'T ANSWER.

GABRIEL, YOU CAN FIND THEM!
YOU FOUND ME WHEN I NEEDED YOU.
I-I CAN'T...

I'M **CONNECTED** TO YOU. **ONLY** TO YOU. I ALWAYS KNOW WHEN YOU **NEED** ME.
IT WAS **SUPPOSED** TO BE JULIA. **THAT'S** WHO I WAS **SENT** HERE FOR!
BUT THAT ALL CHANGED WHEN WE...

JULIA, WHAT'S HE TALKING ABOUT?
MOM, I DON'T HAVE A CLUE.

MAKE YOU SOME TEA, MRS. ALVAREZ? COFFEE? THERE'S SOME BETHANY'S BLEND IN THE KITCHEN. IT'LL HELP YOU CALM DOWN, THINK MORE CLEARLY.
THANK YOU.

COME ON...

YOU CAN HELP JULIA MORE THAN ***I*** COULD...

GLORY, WHAT WAS HE TALKING ABOUT?

WE'LL PHONE BIG AL FROM HERE. HE WON'T RECOGNIZE ***MY*** CALLER ID, SO MAYBE HE'LL ANSWER.
WHAT'S HIS NUMBER?

YEAH, ***SURE*** I KNOW YOU, JULIA'S ***FRIEND,*** RIGHT?
♫ YORE CHEAT HEART. . ♫

NO, HONEY, I CAN'T DO THAT. ESTELLA'S MY ***BABY GIRL,*** AND MY WIFE IS TRYING TO ***KEEP HER FROM ME.***

WHICH IS ***NOT RIGHT.*** I ***GOT*** HER NOW, AND I ***AIN'T*** GIVIN' HER BACK!

SOB

YOU TELL MY WIFE, YOU HEAR? YOU TELL HER IF SHE GETS ANYWHERE NEAR ME--

I HEARD A LOT OF VOICES. AND LOUD COUNTRY-WESTERN MUSIC.
THERE'S THE OKAY CORRAL, A BIKER BAR IN THE MISSION DISTRICT, WHERE HE LIKES TO HANG OUT.

HE TOOK MY ***BABY SISTER*** TO A ***BAR?*** MOM WILL ***KILL HIM!***
THE OKAY CORRAL? I KNOW WHERE THAT IS. I'LL GO TALK TO HIM.

WAIT! WE SHOULD TAKE ***GABRIEL...***
SHH. IF BIG AL SEES ME WITH A STRANGE GUY I BET HE'LL FREAK. HE'LL DEFINITELY FREAK IF I BRING YOU AND YOUR MOM.
DON'T TELL YOUR MOM WHERE I'VE GONE OR ***SHE'LL*** FREAK.

OKAY CORRAL
KATHUMP
KATHUMP

♫...SHOT A MAN IN
JUST
WATCH HIM DIE...♫

UM, MISTER ALVAREZ?
=AHEM=

BIG AL!

YOU TALKIN' TO ME? YOU TALKIN' TO ME?
I'M GLORY? JULIA'S FRIEND? I WAS JUST TALKING TO YOU ON THE PHONE?
SO?
SO I'VE COME TO TAKE ESTELLA BACK TO HER MOTHER?
THUMP

OH MY GOD.

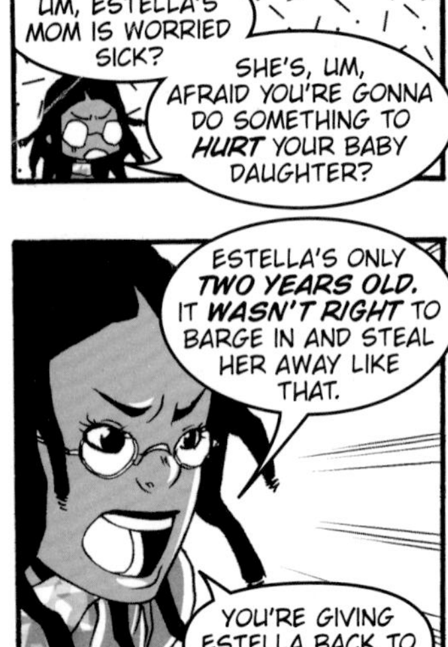

HE'S RIGHT. YOU LISTEN TO THIS KID HERE AND GIVE THAT BABY GIRL BACK TO HER MAMA.

TAKING A LITTLE GIRL AWAY FROM HER MAMA, THAT AIN'T RIGHT.

BABY GIRL **NEEDS** HER MAMA ON CHRISTMAS EVE!

YEAH, YOU SHOULDN'T TAKE NO BABY AWAY FROM NO MAMA. WASSAMATTA, DON'T YOU LOVE YOUR MAMA?

SOB

I DON'T **HAVE** A MOTHER. I DON'T HAVE **ANYONE** ON CHRISTMAS EVE!

YOU GOT **US.**

SHE DIED WHEN I WAS ONLY TWO YEARS OLD. S-SAME AGE AS **ESTELLA.** WE NEVER REALLY H-HAD A CHRISTMAS!

DO THE RIGHT THING, BIG AL.
I'LL TAKE YOU TO ESTELLA.

snf
THIS WAY.

Awwww
Ohhhhh
C'MON OVER TO ME AND MY MAMA'S PLACE FOR CHRISTMAS, MAN.

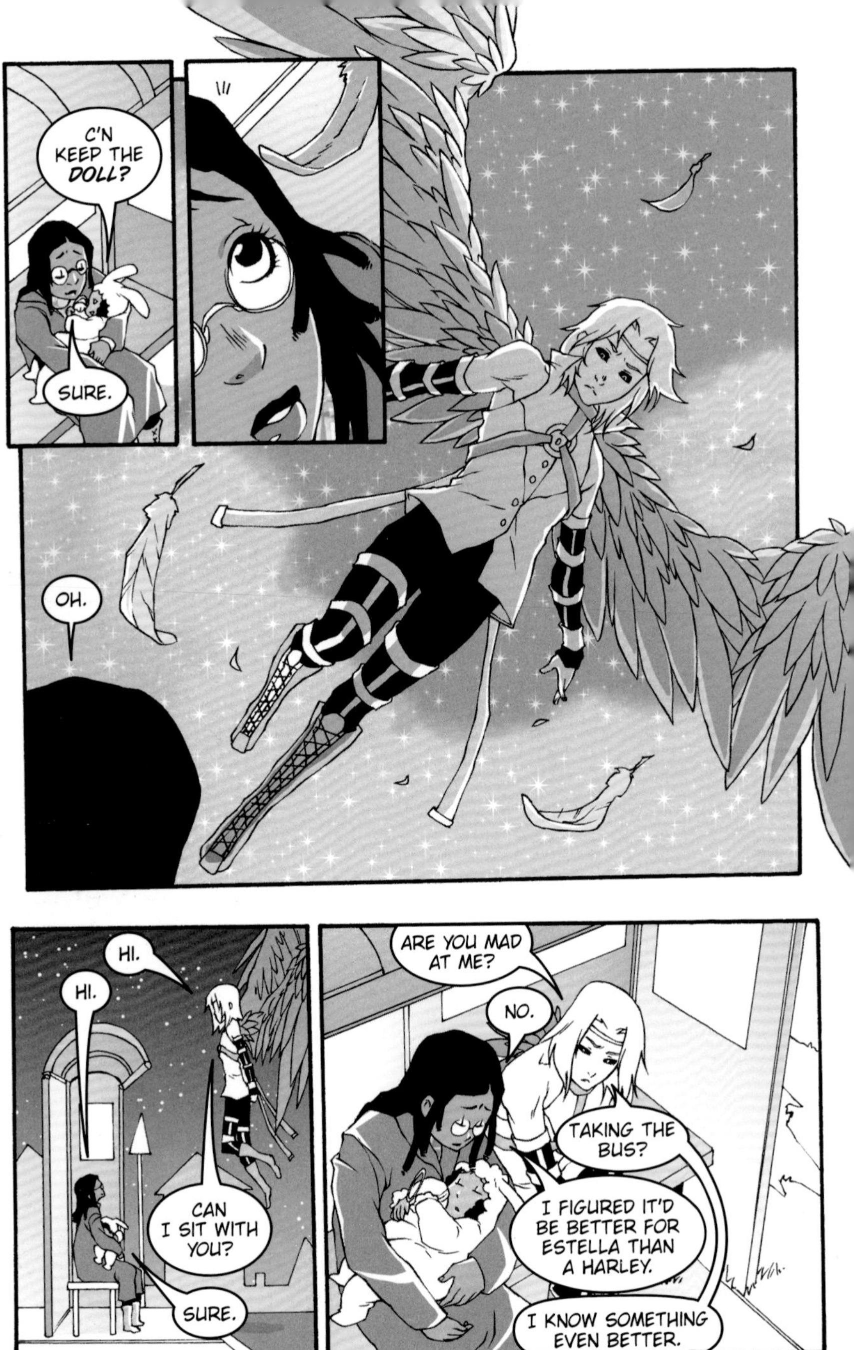

C'N KEEP THE *DOLL?*
SURE.
OH.

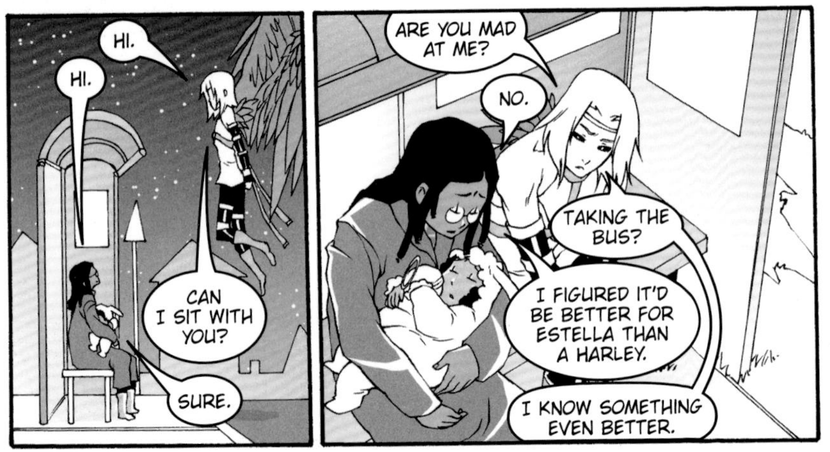

GABRIEL, LOOK!

IT'S CHRISTMAS MORNING!

BUT--

I **KNOW,**
I SHOULDN'T HAVE--

CAN I AT **LEAST**
SAY **GOOD-BYE?**

Sigh

KA CHK
CHK
CHK

GABRIEL, WHAT...? IT'S 6 A.M.

I HAVE TO GO BACK TO WHERE I CAME FROM. I'VE BEEN ORDERED TO LEAVE.
HUH?

MY GUARDIAN IS PRETTY MAD AT ME BECAUSE INSTEAD OF BEING JULIA'S GUARDIAN ANGEL, I MESSED EVERYTHING UP BY FALLING IN LOVE WITH YOU.
BIG AL COULDN'T HAVE TAKEN ESTELLA IF I'D BEEN CONNECTED TO JULIA. HE COULD HAVE OPENED UP TO HIS FAMILY ABOUT HIS MOTHER, IF...
IF I HADN'T PUT MYSELF FIRST.

YOU DIDN'T PUT YOURSELF FIRST. YOU PUT ME FIRST.
EVERYTHING THAT HAPPENED WAS MY FAULT.
BUT IT TURNED OUT OK. YOU WERE RIGHT WHEN YOU SAID I COULD HELP JULIA MORE THAN YOU COULD.
HA! MY GUARDIAN DOESN'T SEE IT THAT WAY.

W-WILL I EVER SEE YOU AGAIN?
NOT SO THAT YOU'D KNOW IT WAS ME.
AND YOU CAN'T SPEND YOUR LIFE WAITING FOR THAT TO HAPPEN.

THAT RINGTONE!

YES, YES, I'M COMING. JUST ONE MORE MINUTE.

QUICK! KISS ME GOOD-BYE!

ANGELS CAN CRY...
GABRIEL?

OH.
MORNING GLORY, WHAT ARE YOU DOING OUTSIDE? COME OPEN YOUR PRESENTS!

ART PENCILS IN ALL THE COLORS IN THE UNIVERSE! THANK YOU!
...JUST THAT HE HAD TO GO BACK TO HIS FAMILY.
A SHAME. HE SEEMED LIKE SUCH A NICE KID.
SHE SEEMS TO BE TAKING IT WELL.

OPEN IT!
FOR ME?

I USED TO WEAR EARRINGS, AND I WAS JUST THINKING OF STARTING AGAIN.
THANK YOU, HONEY!
WAIT, HERE'S ONE MORE PRESENT.
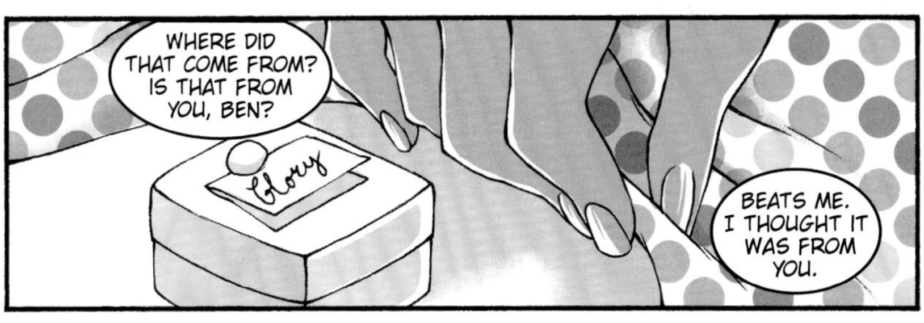
WHERE DID THAT COME FROM? IS THAT FROM YOU, BEN?
Glory
BEATS ME. I THOUGHT IT WAS FROM YOU.

OH, GABRIEL.

Ding!
MUFFINS ARE READY.
COME AND GET IT!

BE RIGHT THERE. I'LL JUST TAKE ALL THIS SWAG TO MY ROOM.

SO BIG AL'S STARTED GOING TO AA MEETINGS AND GROUP THERAPY FOR ANGER MANAGEMENT, AND IN RETURN, MOM ISN'T PRESSING CHARGES.
SOMETIME DOWN THE ROAD SHE'LL LET HIM VISIT ESTELLA-- ***SUPERVISED.***
BUT HE'LL HAVE TO ***REALLY, REALLY*** GET HIS ACT TOGETHER FIRST.
BIO
BUT HOW ABOUT ***YOU?*** I CAN'T BELIEVE GABRIEL ***DUMPED*** YOU LIKE THAT!
HEY!
COMIN' THROUGH.
IT WASN'T ***LIKE*** THAT, JULIA. HE HAD NO CHOICE.
AND I'M OK--
MOVE IT.
BIO
I WILL ***NOT*** MOVE IT! WHAT ARE YOU GONNA ***DO*** ABOUT IT?

I WILL NOT BE BULLIED BY YOU ANYMORE!
YOU ARE OVER!
mutter
mutter
mutter
BIOLOGY
clap
clap
clap

tee hee

AND THE SAME GOES FOR YOU!
YOU CAN KEEP YOUR STUPID CAFETERIA TABLE! I WOULDN'T SIT WITH YOU IF MY LIFE DEPENDED ON IT!
AND PUT SOME CLOTHES ON BEFORE YOU CATCH PNEUMONIA!

clap
clap
clap

I'll miss you, Daisy. You made me a stronger person.
But I must return to my home on the magical island of Catlandia.
This is my gift to you so you never forget me.
I'll never forget you! I'll never love another cat!
no this is stupid it's not working

Hi, Glory.

My name is Dylan Ruiz. I don't know if yo
remember me, but I sat next to you at Yaek
Fujimoto's comics workshop last week. I rea
liked your comic, and I was wondering if you
like to work on a comic with me. We could
take turns penciling and inking and get it don
in time for next year's D.O.G. Festival. I live in
Berkeley, but I don't mind taking the train to
San Francisco. Would you be interested?

HI DYLAN,
I REMEMBER YOU, AND THAT SOUNDS LIKE FUN! I THINK I ALREADY HAVE AN IDEA. IT'D BE GREAT TO HAVE SOMEONE TO WORK ON IT WITH.

I WANT TO DO A COMIC ABOUT AN ANGEL.

The Sunset Sunrise

DEAR GLORY

Sunrise High School is proud to present a new advice column from senior student Morning Glory Conroy. Last year, Ms. Conroy was nominated for an award in the category of "best new graphic novel by an artist under the age of 18." Her almost-prize-winning memoir, *I Touched an Angel*, cowritten with her boyfriend, Dylan Ruiz, is soon to be published.

The editorial staff here at THE SUNSET SUNRISE feel that, as someone who has suffered the slings and arrows of having a very unusual boyfriend, Ms. Conroy is uniquely qualified to advise others on their problems with usual and unusual girlfriends and boyfriends or either or both.

Dear Glory,

You may have had the same problem I'm having. My boyfriend's an angel too, and we're engaged to be married. To start with, my mom is dead set against him. She says, "How will he support you?" and "What kind of life will you have, with him flying off all the time?" I think we can deal with all of those problems when the time comes, but right now: he's molting! Maybe it's the season or something, but there are feathers all over my house. I'm cleaning up after him all the time, and feathers clog the vacuum cleaner. They also get in your nose. Mom is sneezing all the time and is getting pretty ticked off. What can I do?

Signed,
Buried in Fluff

Dear Buried,

I'm sorry to say that Gabriel didn't stick around long enough to molt. Have you

thought of putting those feathers to use? Instead of vacuuming them up, start collecting them, and soon you will have enough to stuff a pillow, maybe two. Angel feathers are softer than even goose feathers, which cost a fortune. Soon you may even have enough for a comforter—and all free! When you give your mother a pillow set and matching comforter, she can't help but be impressed, and will give you both her blessing.

Dear Glory,

I've fallen in love with the new girl behind the counter at Bethany's Coffee, but she won't give me the time of day. Trouble is, the only time I ever saw her smile was when she poured tabasco sauce into somebody's coffee. I think she hates her job. I have dared to suggest that she could look for another one, but she says she did something wrong last year and working all her spare time at Bethany's is her punishment. How can I help her?

Signed,
Eating donuts in the Sunset

Dear Eating,

Uh-oh! I suggest you run the other way, fast. If you still crave donuts and coffee, I can recommend a different Bethany's in the Mission District.

Dear Glory,

You probably feel pretty rotten about me, because of how I harassed you last year when we were both juniors. But now that I'm a senior, I'm really sorry. I'm just so in love with Madame Baaaad. She's all I think about all the time, and I dream about her at night. I know she could lay me out cold with one swipe of her fist, but I don't care. She's the kind of girl who won't put up with any dumb junior messing her around. I love her!

Signed,
Mario el Magnifico

Dear Mario,

A year is a long time, and all that stuff is water under the bridge, so forget it. In the meantime, there are a lot of very nice girls at Sunset High School. Most of them don't look like Madame Baaaad, but some of them are just as tough. Give them a chance!

ABOUT THE AUTHOR AND THE ARTISTS

TRINA ROBBINS established herself during the underground comix movement of the 1960s and in the 1970s published the first all-woman comic book—*It Ain't Me, Babe Comix*—and the anthology *Wimmen's Comix*. She was a penciller on Wonder Woman in the 1980s, created the series Go Girl! with artist Anne Timmons for Image Comics, has written numerous nonfiction books for children and adults, and designed Vampirella's costume. She is the author of the Graphic Universe series Chicagoland Detective Agency. She lives in San Francisco with her partner, comics artist Steve Leialoha.

XIAN NU STUDIO (Irene Diaz Miranda and Laura Moreno Fernandez) published their first manga in 2007. Then they continued with *All In*, a three-volume manga about poker for Les Humanoïdes Associés in France. In 2008 they illustrated Melissa Marr's trilogy *Wicked Lovely: Desert Tales* for TokyoPop, coedited by HarperCollins, followed up by their creator-owned series, Bakemono. They live in Granada, Spain, enjoying the sun whenever they're not rushing to meet a deadline.

YUKO OTA, creator of the popular webcomic series Johnny Wander with writer Ananth Panagariya, has worked as an animator and a lab assistant but is happiest drawing creatures and inventing worlds. She draws on the subway, in coffee shops, on the living room couch, and in her cozy home office somewhere in Brooklyn, New York.